NOBODY'S PERFECT

David Elliott

ILLUSTRATED BY **Sam Zuppardi**

Candlewick Press

"Nobody's perfect."

That's what everybody says.
And I guess they're right.

Like Gigi.
She's my sister.

She's not perfect.

She's loud!

Or my best friend, Jack.

He's kind of a show-off.
Not perfect!

And even my mom.

She gave me a time-out.
That's why I'm
sitting on this step . . .

even though it's
not my fault that
Ralphie likes to sleep
on my bed.

I've told her a million times.
Ralphie should get a time-out.
Not me.

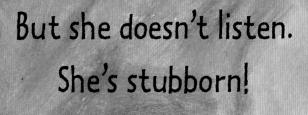

But she doesn't listen.
She's stubborn!

And
that's
not
perfect.

I'm not perfect, either.

This is my room
before I clean it.

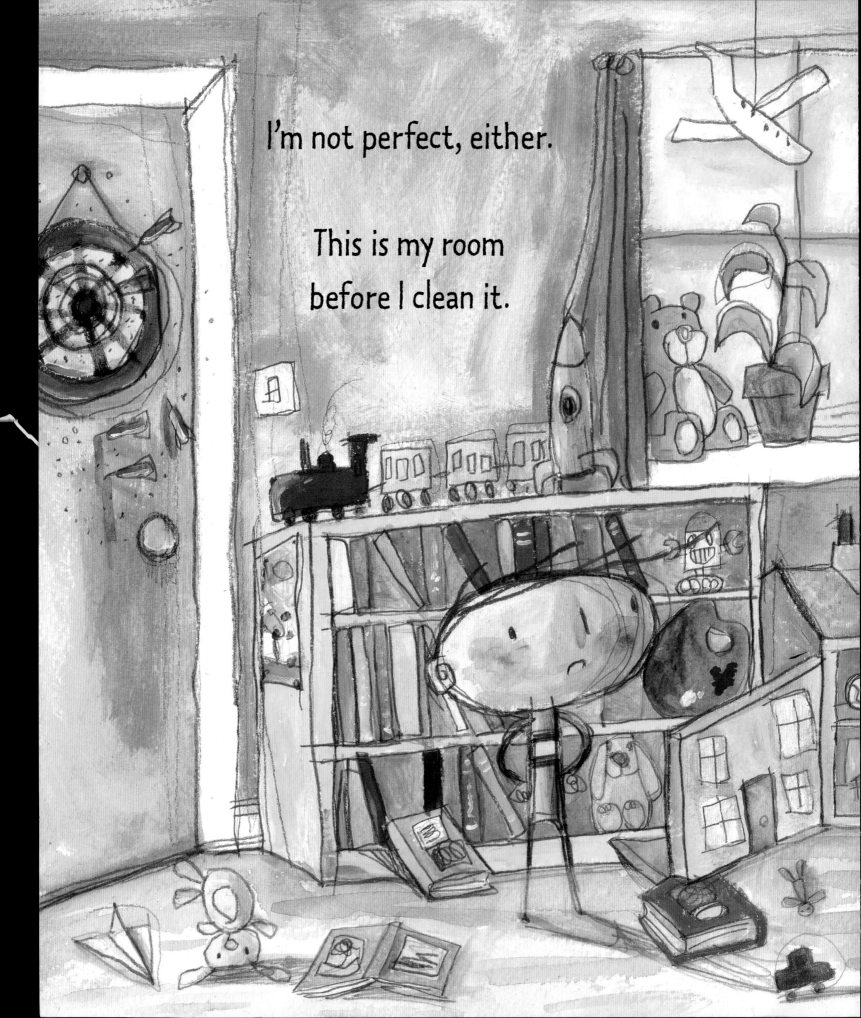

This is my room
after I clean it.

But sometimes I *have* to be messy.

And sometimes it's fun
when Jack shows off.

And sometimes I'm happy
that Gigi is loud.

Really loud!

And even my mom.
Sometimes she does listen.

And when she does . . .

it's perfect.

No, nobody's perfect.

But sometimes
they come close . . .

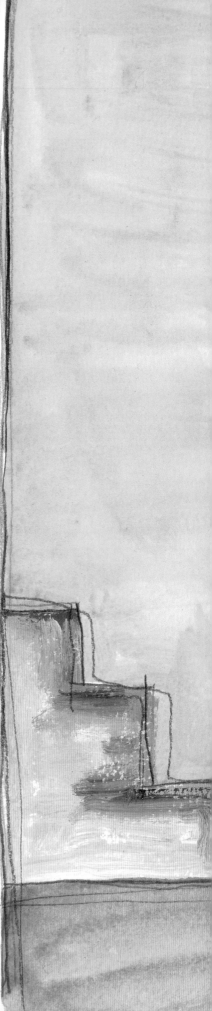

and that's perfect
enough for me.

To Susan Goodman, a perfect friend
D. E.

For Mum
S. Z.

Text copyright © 2015 by David Elliott
Illustrations copyright © 2015 by Sam Zuppardi

First edition 2015

Library of Congress Catalog Card Number 2013957285
ISBN 978-0-7636-6699-6

14 15 16 17 18 19 CCP 10 9 8 7 6 5 4 3 2 1

Printed in Shenzhen, Guangdong, China

This book was typeset in Kosmik.
The illustrations were done in acrylic paint and pencil
on watercolor paper.

Candlewick Press
99 Dover Street
Somerville, Massachusetts 02144

visit us at www.candlewick.com